Usborne

Illustrated

Animal
Stories

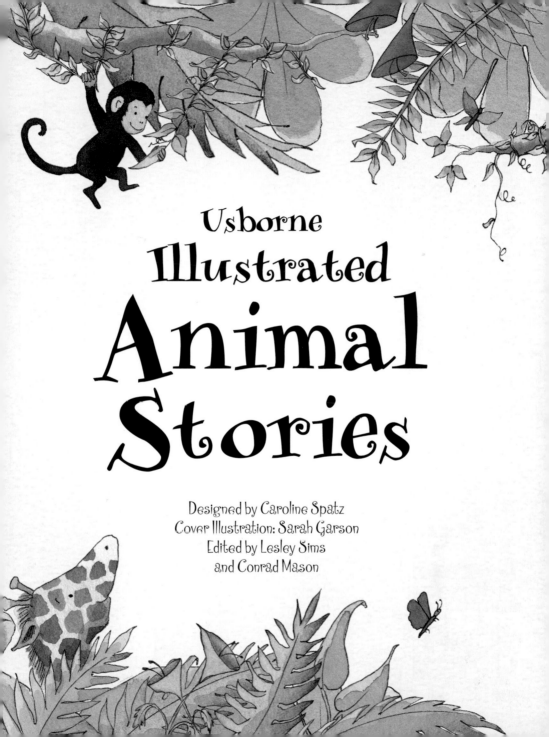

Usborne
Illustrated
Animal
Stories

Designed by Caroline Spatz
Cover Illustration: Sarah Garson
Edited by Lesley Sims
and Conrad Mason

CONTENTS

The Musicians of Bremen

Near the town of Bremen, there once lived
a very mean farmer...

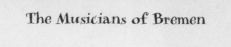

He had lots of animals on his farm, and he was mean to them all.

He made his donkey carry heavy loads from dawn until dusk.

Hurry up you lazy beast!

And he flew into a rage
if it tripped or stumbled.

He fed his dog scraps while he and his wife devoured tasty pies and crisp, golden roasts.

Here, you greedy thing.

And, when it rained, he kicked his cat outside, and left it shivering in the cold.

One day,
the rooster
overheard the
farmer talking.

"That rooster's too old," he said to his wife. "We'll put him in the pot and eat him for lunch."

And he licked his lips.

I'll get him tomorrow.

That evening, the rooster stood on a fence and crowed as hard as he could.

"What are you doing?" asked the donkey.

14

"I'm crowing for the last time," sobbed
the rooster, telling his friends about the
farmer's plans to eat him.

Tomorrow I'll be
rooster stew.

"This time he's gone too far!" said the donkey. "I'm not going to let that mean farmer make a meal of you!"

"Why don't we run away?" the cat piped up. "I know just where we can go..."

"To Bremen! We can be musicians and join the town band."

The four friends thought it was an
excellent idea, and they set off at once.

They walked and walked, until
they came to a thick, dark forest.

"We'll have to sleep here tonight," said the donkey. No one was very happy about that.

"Wait!" crowed the rooster. "I can see a light."

They crept closer. The light was coming from a little cottage.

"But who could live here, right in the middle of the forest?" said the dog.

The donkey peered inside.

"Well? What do you
see?" the dog barked.
"Yes, what?"
asked the others.

23

"Mmm, food and drink!" said the donkey, his stomach rumbling.

Oooh!

"And, um...
a gang of robbers."

Oh!

"How can we get that food?" wailed the dog.

"I think I know..." said the donkey.

The others gathered around to listen to his plan.

Then the donkey
stood next to the
window.

The dog leaped onto
the donkey's back.

The cat jumped on
top of the dog.

And the rooster
flew on top of
the cat.

"Is everyone ready?"
whispered the donkey.
"One... two... three... Go!"

Braying, barking, squealing and squawking, the donkey, the dog, the cat and the rooster BURST inside!

And they bolted out of the door, and ran off into the night.

The four
friends ate...

and ate...

...and ate
some more.

When they had finished,
they were so full, they
each found a comfy spot
and went to sleep.

37

Meanwhile, the robbers were watching
the house.

"We shouldn't have run away,"
growled the leader. "Someone should go
in there and see what's going on."

"Come here little robber," he called to
the smallest robber. "Now," he ordered,
"go back and find out what those
creatures are up to."

Trembling with fear, the smallest robber crept into the kitchen. The house was silent and dark, except for the shining eyes of the cat.

"Ah ha! Burning coals," thought the smallest robber. "I'll use them to light a candle. Then I'll see what's going on."
    And he bent down to the fireplace...

But as soon as he put his candle near the cat's eyes...

...she leaped straight for his face.

Aaaagh!

Terrified, the robber ran to the door...

...where the dog bit his leg.

The poor robber flew out of the door, and raced across the yard. He was so busy trying to escape, that he ran straight into...

...the donkey.

"What took you so long?" grumbled the leader, when the smallest robber returned.

"There's a horrible witch in there," he panted. "When I tried to light my candle, she spat at me and scratched me with her claws."

"And by the door there's a huge man with a sword. He stabbed me in the leg. Look!" He showed them his leg, where the dog had bitten him. "But worst of all," he went on...

"There's a big, black monster in the yard. He beat me with his club."

The robber leader turned a sickly shade of green. "Let's get out of here," he said nervously, "before they come looking for us!"

The robbers never went back
to the house again.

And as
for the four
friends...

...they never did go to Bremen
to become musicians.

They liked the robbers' house so
much that they stayed there for the
rest of their lives.

Chicken Licken

There was once a farm where all the
animals were happy, except one...

Chicken Licken

Chicken Licken
had a problem. He was
afraid – of everything.

He was scared of the tiniest mouse...

...the friendliest worm...

Help! ...and even his own shadow.

One day, Chicken Licken went for a walk in the woods. He darted from tree to tree, looking out for anything scary.

After a while, he sat down for a rest under a great oak tree.

At that moment, a tiny acorn dropped
from the tree, and fell to the ground...

...where it hit Chicken Licken on the head.

Bonk!

Chicken Licken sat up at once, and opened his eyes wide.

He didn't see the acorn behind him. He had no idea what could have hit him.

What was that?

Chicken Licken looked up at the blue sky above and gasped.

"Oh no," he thought. "It must be the sky. The sky is falling!"

He ran around the tree in a panic.
"The sky is falling! The sky is falling!"
he cried. "I must tell everyone at once."

"And of course, the King will want to hear of this," he thought, puffing out his chest importantly.

Back at the farm, Henny Penny
was sitting by the hen house, when
Chicken Licken raced by.

"Out of my way!"
yelled Chicken Licken.

"What's the matter?" asked
Henny Penny.

"The sky is falling!" cried Chicken
Licken. "I've got to warn everybody."

"Oh no!" said Henny Penny.
"What should we do?"

"We have to tell the King," said
Chicken Licken. "He'll know."

So off they went.

They ran past the hen house and
into the farmyard, where...

Thump! They bumped
straight into Cocky Locky.

"Hey! Watch where you're going,"
said Cocky Locky.

"But the sky is falling!"
cried Chicken Licken.

69

"Good grief!" said Cocky Locky.
"We must do something."

"We are," said Henny Penny. "We're going to tell the King."

"That's a splendid idea," said Cocky Locky. "I'll come too."

And they all set off together.

Soon, they passed the duck pond, where Ducky Lucky was enjoying a morning swim.

"What's got your feathers in such a flap?" he quacked.

"The sky is falling!" cried Chicken Licken.

73

"That's terrible!" said Ducky
Lucky. "What are we going to do?"

"We're going to tell the King," said
Cocky Locky. "Why don't you come too?"

74

"I think I'd better," said Ducky Lucky.

And they ran across the bridge.

Before long, they came to the old barn, where Goosey Loosey was sitting quietly on her nest.

"What's the matter?" she honked, when she saw them all hurrying along.

"The sky is falling! The sky is falling!"
cried Chicken Licken.

"The sky is falling?" gasped Goosey Loosey. "Does the King know about this?"

"We're off to tell him right now," panted Ducky Lucky.

"Wait for me!" called Goosey Loosey.

And they set off once again.

At last, they reached the field beyond the farm. Turkey Lurkey was looking for worms.

"What's the matter, Chicken Licken?" she asked.

"It looks like you're
in quite a hurry."

"The sky is falling!"
cried Chicken Licken.

"Is it true?" spluttered
Turkey Lurkey.

"Yes! Yes!" everyone clucked,
squawked or quacked.

"There's not a moment to lose.
We're going to tell the King."

82

"This is serious," said Turkey
Lurkey, bringing up the rear.

And they ran on
through the field.

83

Soon they came to the forest, where Foxy Loxy lived.

"What are you all doing here, so far from the farm?" asked Foxy Loxy.

84

"The sky is falling!"
cried Chicken Licken.

"Really," said Foxy Loxy and smiled to
himself. What nonsense! The sky couldn't
possibly be falling. But he didn't say that...

85

"We're going to tell the King," said Turkey Lurkey. "Why don't you come too?"

"I think I will," said Foxy Loxy, with a smirk. "I know a shortcut we can take."

He led them deeper and deeper into the forest...

...until they reached a hole.
"It's down here,"
he said.

Henny Penny looked puzzled as she followed the others. "Is this where the King lives?" she asked.

"No," said Foxy Loxy. "It's where I live. And it's where I'm going to gobble you all up!"

He licked his lips and got ready to pounce.

"But if you gobble us up," said Chicken Licken, "who will tell the King that the sky is falling?"

"You stupid bird," said Foxy Loxy. "The sky isn't falling."

No sooner had he spoken, than an acorn fell from a tree, and hit Foxy Loxy on the head.

Foxy Loxy didn't see the acorn.
All he could see was the sky.
He started to tremble.

The sky is
falling!

Now it was Foxy Loxy who
was scared.

With a worried cry, he jumped
down the tunnel and ran for his life.

He was never seen again.

Now, the others had seen the
acorn fall on Foxy Loxy's head.
They all glared at Chicken Licken.

"Are you *quite* sure it was the sky
that fell on your head?" they said.

"Umm... Maybe it was an acorn," said Chicken Licken, looking embarrassed.

"Chicken Licken!" they yelled, and they chased him all the way back to the farm.

The Fox and the Crow

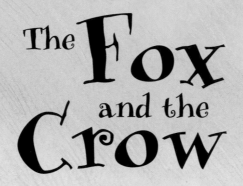

Fox was the craftiest creature in the woods, and he always got his way.

One day, while Fox was out strolling, he saw Crow perched high up in her nest. She was clutching a large lump of cheese in her beak.

Mmm, that smells good!

As soon as he saw the cheese,
Fox wanted it for himself. So he
thought of a way to get it.

"My, how pretty you are!"
he said, smiling up at Crow.

Me?

Crow was delighted with the compliment. "I suppose I am rather pretty!" she thought to herself.

"And what lovely, glossy feathers you have!" Fox went on. "I do believe you are the prettiest bird I've ever seen."

Crow spread her
wings proudly, and
strutted along a branch.

103

Fox smiled.
His plan was
working...

Then he sighed. "If only you could sing," he said, "you would be the most wonderful creature that I've ever met."

"Really?" thought Crow.
"Wait until he hears this!"

CAW!

She opened her beak to sing,
and let out a horrible squawk.
At once, the lump of cheese
dropped from her mouth.

It plummeted down...

"Hey, that was mine!" said
Crow, crossly. "And anyway,
what about my singing?"

But Fox
just laughed.

"Don't always believe people who say nice things," he said. "Sometimes they just want something from you."

And with that,
he trotted away,
chuckling to himself.

The Billy Goats Gruff

Once upon a time, in a faraway
land, there lived three billy goats.

The billy goats were brothers, and their last name was Gruff.

We're the Gruff brothers.

They lived on a farm, in the shadow of a mountain.

Beanie was the youngest. He was small and skinny, always hungry...

Watch out!

and always in trouble.

Bertie was the middle brother.

He was crazy about sports.

Biffer was the oldest. He was big and strong and looked after his brothers.

One winter, there was very little food on the farm.

I'm so hungry!

"I've only eaten a piece of hay today," moaned Beanie.

"Fibber," said Bertie, "You ate two socks and a shirt from the clothesline."

Biffer was worried. "I think it's time we made a move," he said. "We'll starve if we stay here."

"Where will we go?" asked Beanie.

"To the Juicy Fields over the hills," Biffer replied. "There's plenty of food there. We just have to cross the Rushing River."

Bertie looked terrified. "We can't go over the river!" he cried. "That's where the Terrible Troll lives. He'll eat us up."

He's got eyes like saucers.

And a nose as long as a poker!

"Don't be silly," Biffer said. "There's no such thing as trolls. That's farmyard talk."

Just think of the Juicy Fields...

123

The Billy Goats Gruff spent a week preparing for their trip. Biffer found an old map to show them the way.

Then Beanie and Bertie had
to learn to climb up hills.

Beanie was
better at coming
down.

Ooph!

But after a few days, they were both excellent climbers.

Finally, the brothers had to pack for their journey.

At last, they were ready to leave.

Good luck!

Bye Beanie!
Don't forget us.

A chick and a piglet wanted to go too,
but the older animals shook their heads.

"Let's hope they make it past the
bridge," they muttered.

129

Bertie and Beanie were dreaming of
the Juicy Fields as they left the farm.

The Dark Forest loomed ahead.

"I'm not sure I want to go in there," said Beanie.

"We'll be fine," said Biffer, "as long as we stick together."

Suddenly, a thick mist swirled around them.

I can hardly see
my feet.

Beanie shivered. "I don't like this forest," he said, "it's spooky. Do you think there might be ghosts here?"

"Yes," said Bertie, with a grin. "Lots of ghosts. And more than anything, ghosts like scaring little billy goats."

Whoooooo!

Argh!

"That's enough, Bertie," said Biffer sternly. "Stop scaring Beanie."

The billy goats walked on in silence.
"Um, Biffer?" said Beanie, after a while.
"Yes, Beanie?"
"I think someone's following
us. Listen."

The billy goats stopped to listen... and
heard a thumping sound. It grew louder.

"Look!" shrieked Beanie. A strange shape was coming down the path, and it was heading straight for them.

"It's a ghost!" cried Beanie. "Run! Run for your lives."

Before Biffer could stop them, Beanie and Bertie had raced off down the path.

We've got to stick together!

"Come back," Biffer shouted. "It can't be a ghost. It's a..."

Biffer waited, as the shape appeared from the mist. "It's just a rabbit," he said.

"I'm not *just* a rabbit," said the rabbit. "I'm a rare breed of tall, lop-eared rabbit and my name is Buffy."

"I'm Biffer. Nice to meet you," said
Biffer, "but I must find my brothers before
they get lost."

"Where are you going?" Buffy asked.
"To the Juicy Fields," Biffer called, as
he ran after his brothers.

"Watch out for the troll," Buffy shouted after him. But Biffer had already gone.

Oh dear. No one's ever made it past the troll.

Hello? Anyone
there?

Meanwhile, Bertie was wandering
alone through the forest – totally lost.

Beanie had been luckier. He had found the path that ran straight through the forest.

Whew! That was close.

"I can't wait to get to the Juicy Fields," Beanie thought, as he trotted along.

Before long he came to the bridge over the Rushing River. Next to the bridge was a big wooden sign.

"I wish I could read," thought Beanie.

His hooves went clippety-clop, clippety-clop over the bridge. But as he reached the middle of the river...

Help!

...a large, muddy hand smashed through the wooden planks and grabbed his leg.

"Who's that clippety-clopping over my bridge?" roared a terrible voice. "I'm coming to gobble you up!"

Let go!

Beanie's eyes bulged with terror. There, poking his head through the bridge, was a fat and warty troll.

"Please don't eat me," cried Beanie. "My big brother will be crossing soon. He's much bigger and tastier than me."

I'm sure you'd rather eat him.

"I think I can wait a little longer for my dinner," said the troll. "Now scram!"

Shaking with fear, Beanie wobbled off the bridge and hid in some bushes. "I hope Bertie can save himself," he thought.

Bertie arrived soon after and trotted
onto the bridge, bouncing his ball –
clappety-clop-bonk, clappety-clop-bonk.

"Who's that bouncing over my bridge?" bellowed the troll.

Oh no!

Bertie gulped. "I didn't think trolls were real," he said.

"I'm real and I'm hungry," said the troll, "and I'm coming to gobble you up!"

But I don't want to be dinner.

"You'll make a tasty meal," he added. "Nice fresh billy goat. Yum, yum."

"Stop!" cried Bertie, thinking quickly. "You can't eat me. My big brother is coming behind me. He's much fatter."

What big teeth you have...

"Humph," said the troll, pausing mid-pounce. "I'll wait for the fattest one then. He'd better be juicy."

I'm getting hungrier...

At last, Biffer came out of the forest.
He soon spotted his brothers on the other
side of the river, and raced to the bank.

Beanie and Bertie leaped out of the bushes, waving their hooves wildly.

"Stop Biffer!" they cried. "STOP! There's a troll under the bridge."

It was too late. Biffer was already crossing. His heavy hooves went clunkety-clop, clunkety-clop and the bridge strained under his weight.

By this time, the troll was starving.

"Who's that stomping over my bridge?" he roared.

I'm going to gobble you up!

But Biffer wasn't scared. "I'm an enormous billy goat," he said, "and I'm ready for a fight."

155

Biffer bounced the troll into the air. Then, with a toss of his horns, he whacked him into the Rushing River.

The troll sank under
the water and was never seen again.

Beanie and Bertie couldn't believe it. "You're the best, Biffer!" they cried.

Just then, a stream of animals came out of the forest, and skipped over the bridge.

"Where are you going?" Biffer asked a rabbit.

"To the Juicy Fields!" she replied. "We've been trapped in the forest for years, because of the troll. Now, thanks to you, we're free."

I hope there'll be enough food!

The Leopard
and
the Sky God

Long ago, when the world was young,
the Sky God ruled over all things...

161

He lived high up in the clouds,
and he watched over all the
animals of the earth.

He looked after them
both day and night.

The Sky God loved all the animals. But it was lonely in the clouds, and sometimes he got a little bored.

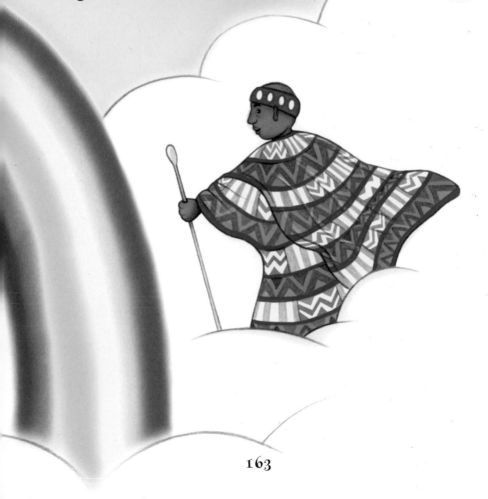

One day, the Sky God heard a wonderful sound drifting up from the forest below.

He leaned over the edge of his cloud and peered through the trees, to see where the sound was coming from.

And there in a clearing, he spotted the leopard, playing a big drum.

Where did he get that?

The Sky God was entranced. He had never seen such a beautiful drum. And what a sound it made!

The leopard was having the time of his life.

He played the drum *high*

and low,

He played it softly,

and he played it
loud!

The Sky God floated gently down on a
cloud, and stepped onto the grass. "Hello,
Leopard," he smiled.

"That's a fine drum you have.
May I please have a turn?"
    But the leopard
frowned.

"No," said the leopard, clutching his drum tightly. "I made it all by myself, and I'm the only one who's allowed to play it."

Go away!

The Sky God was disappointed. "I promise I'll be very careful," he said.

Come on, share it.

"No!" said the leopard crossly. And he ran away, taking his drum with him.

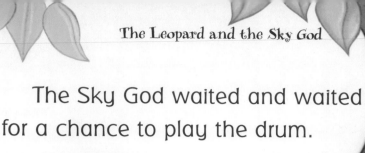

The Sky God waited and waited for a chance to play the drum.

He hoped to borrow it when the leopard went hunting.

But the leopard took the drum with him wherever he went, and he guarded it the whole time. He was determined not to share it with anyone.

After a week, the Sky God called the other animals together.

"What's the matter?" they asked. So the Sky God told them all about the leopard and his drum.

I just wish I could try that drum.

"I'll talk to the leopard,"
said the python.

"Maybe I can perssssssuade him to
ssshare hisssss drum with you."

The python slithered off, and soon found the leopard sitting in his clearing. As usual, the leopard was playing his drum. The python smiled.

Hello, Leopard.

"What do you want?" growled the leopard. He was feeling particularly grumpy, and he didn't like being interrupted when he was playing.

"May I look at your beautiful drum?"
asked the python, sweetly.

"NO!" roared
the leopard.

And he showed his teeth
and sharp claws.

Leave me
alone!

The python slithered away
as quickly as she could.

When she got back, the python
told the Sky God what had
happened.

"Ssssorry," she hissed.

The Sky God sighed. "Will anyone
else help me?" he wondered.

I will!

"I'm not scared of that silly leopard,"
trumpeted the elephant. "I'll talk to him.
He'll give up his drum in no time."

Long before the elephant reached the clearing, he heard the drum. But there was no sign of the leopard.

He looked around. Then he spotted
the leopard, sitting up in a tree. He was
playing his drum and grinning to himself.

"Good afternoon, Leopard," said the elephant politely. "May I please look at your drum?"

But this time, the leopard was in an even worse mood.

"Leave me in peace!" he roared.
And he kept on playing.

"Very well," said the elephant. "I'll soon have you down from there." And he began to shake the tree as hard as he could.

After a while, his head began to hurt, but he couldn't shake the leopard out. Finally, he gave up.

"Well?" said the Sky God, hopefully.

"Sorry," said the elephant.

It's too difficult.

The Sky God was about to give up all together, when a little voice spoke.

"Let me try," said the tortoise.

Now in those days the tortoise had
no shell, only a soft small body.
When they heard the tortoise offer
to help, all the other animals began
to laugh.

You?

"What can you do?" they chorused, still chortling.

But the tortoise smiled. "Wait and see," she said.

So the tortoise went to find the
leopard. He was still sitting in the tree,
with his beloved drum in his paws.
The tortoise smiled up at him.

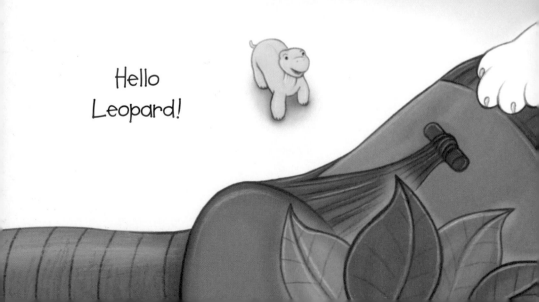

Hello
Leopard!

"Have you seen the Sky God's drum?" she asked.

"The Sky God doesn't have a drum,"
said the puzzled leopard. "I'm the only
one who has a drum around here."
But all the same, he was
very curious.

Oh yes
he does.

"It's the biggest drum I've ever seen,"
said the tortoise. "Much bigger than
yours. The Sky God's drum is so big that
he can climb all the way inside it."

"My drum is the biggest drum!" the leopard bellowed. "And I'll prove it!"

Swiftly, he climbed down from the tree.

The leopard lay his drum on its side and crawled in. "This will be easy," he boasted.

Watch this!

"But can you get ALL the way in?" said the tortoise. Three mischievous monkeys paused to watch.

"Of course I can," scoffed the leopard, creeping in further.

Meanwhile, the tortoise looked around and noticed the leopard's cooking pot.

Quickly, she grabbed the lid and
clapped it over the end of the drum, with
the leopard trapped inside. "Ha, got you!"
said the tortoise.

With the monkeys' help, she rolled the drum along the ground, all the way back to the Sky God, while the leopard groaned inside.

The leopard staggered out feeling dizzy and sick. "I don't want it anymore," he said. "You can have it."

The Sky God cheered. "It's mine!" he cried. "Now, tortoise, what can I give you as a reward?"

"Well, Sky God," said the tortoise, "seeing the leopard in the drum has given me an idea..."

"I think I'd like a shell on my body, just like that drum, so that nothing can ever hurt me."

"Yes, of course," said the Sky God. "Anything you want."

He waved his hands, and at once the tortoise had a hard, green shell on her back. The tortoise was delighted. "Thank you!" she said and plodded away.

The Sky God was thrilled with his drum.

When the weather is stormy, you can still hear him playing it...

playing high and low,

playing soft and **loud!**

The Rescue Dogs

Times were hard for Mr. Tike,
owner of Tike's Dogs' Home.

Things were so bad that Mr. Tike
couldn't afford to repair the creaking old
building. So he was selling it, along with
all the dogs. He gave a sad sigh as he
nailed up a FOR SALE sign.

Inside the home, the dogs were sad too. Mr.Tike had rescued them all and given them a safe place to live.

"I wonder who the new owner will be," woofed Bob the collie.

"I hope they'll be as nice as Mr.Tike," yelped Pip the pointer.

A few days later, two strangers arrived at Tike's.

Hello, I'm Mrs. Hood.

And I'm Mr. Wink.

Tike's Dogs' Home

"We want to buy your sweet little doggy home," said Mrs. Hood.

Mr. Tike showed them around.

In the yard, the dogs rushed up to greet the visitors.

"You let the mutts, er, 1 mean, dogs run around?" asked Mr.Wink.

"Of course," replied Mr.Tike.

"How charming," said Mrs. Hood, with a sickly smile.

In less than a week, the new owners had taken over.

Bye bye Mr. Tike!

"Now then," scowled Mrs. Hood, as soon as Mr. Tike had gone. "Let's get these hairy fleabags out of the way."

Mr.Wink rounded up the dogs. They yelped and barked as he locked them in a cage.

Now we can get to work.

"What's going on?" Heidi the dachshund asked the others.

"Mr.Tike never treated us like this," said Winnie the bulldog.

"We have to get out," said Pip.

"Let me try," said Heidi. Taking a deep breath, she squeezed out of the cage.

"Grab the keys!" called Bob.

Heidi climbed onto a kennel and jumped up to the keys.

214

She freed the others and they ran into the house. On the table they found a scrapbook.

"Hood and Wink are bank robbers!" gasped Bob.

Just then, the dogs heard the pair talking in the yard.

"Remember when this was a field?" Mrs. Hood was saying.

"It was the perfect place to bury our loot."

216

"If only they hadn't built this stinking dog house on top, while we were in jail," moaned Mr.Wink.

"We'll have to bulldoze it to dig up the money. Hey, where are those mutts?"

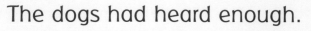

The dogs had heard enough.
Winnie leapt onto Mr.
Wink's head...

...Pip bit
him on the
bottom...   Ooww!

...and Heidi
tugged on
his leg.

Tina the terrier grabbed Mrs. Hood's necklace...

Aagh!

...Bob sank his teeth into her jacket...

...and the Pekingese twins nipped her ankles.

219

Dot the Dalmatian fired chunky dog food into the crooks' faces.

"Run for it!" yelled Mr. Wink.

The dogs chased the two of them out of the home and down the road.

The smell of meaty chunks soon had every dog in town on the villains' trail.

They chased the crooks all the way to the steps of the local police station. Then they stood and barked for help.

What's all this then?

We give in.

The police gave the reward money for catching Hood and Wink to Mr. Tike. And he knew just what to spend it on...

The
Little
Giraffe

Once upon a time, a very long time
ago, a little giraffe lived in East Africa.

This little giraffe was the first giraffe in the world. He would roam the plains...

...with the zebras, the elephants and
the antelopes – though he didn't get too
close to the lions.

The Little Giraffe

But his best friend in the whole world was Rhino.

Every day,
they would tell each
other dreams and secrets.

229

The Little Giraffe

And, every day, they would look for food, in the dusty red sand of the scorching plains.

But the sun blazed down...

...cracking the earth and withering any plants that tried to grow.

I'm hungry.

Often, there was no food
to be found anywhere.

One morning, Rhino's belly rumbled
like a herd of stampeding elephants.
"I'm so hungry," he moaned.

"Perhaps the wise man in the village
can help us," suggested the little giraffe.

They trekked all the way to the
village and called for the wise man.
Leaning on a stick, he came out of his
hut to see what the noise was about.

We're always
hungry.

Please can
you help?

"Hmm," said the wise man, going
back inside his hut to check a potion.

"If you come here again tomorrow, I'll see what I can do."

The next day, the little giraffe visited the wise man on his own. There was no sign of Rhino. The little giraffe hadn't been able to find him anywhere.

"I've made you a magic drink," said the wise man. "But where's your friend?"

The little giraffe had no idea.

"Oh well," said the wise man, "would you like to try it anyway?"

239

The little giraffe began to drink.

First, his legs grew longer...

Then, his neck
s-t-r-e-t-c-h-e-d
up, higher...
   and higher...

"It worked!" cried the wise man.
"Now you can reach the leaves on the
top-most branches of trees."

Meanwhile, where *was* Rhino? Well, he had forgotten all about going to see the wise man, because he had found a tasty patch of dry grass.

He munched away, feeling very pleased with himself.

"*There* you are," said
the not-so-little giraffe,
coming up behind him.
"Hey! What happened
to you?" asked Rhino,
with his mouth full.

You've been
stretched!

243

"The wise man made an amazing magic drink," replied the not-so-little giraffe. "And I grew... and grew... and grew!"

"I wonder what will happen to me?" said Rhino, excitedly.

But there was no drink left. Rhino was furious. "You could have saved me some," he snorted.

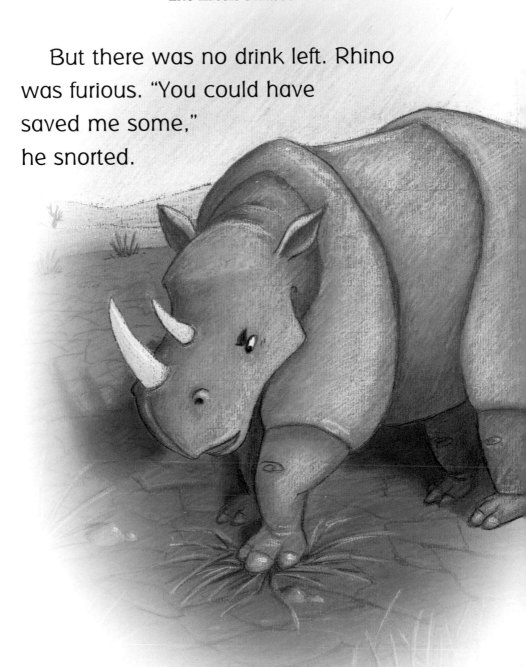

He glared at the
giraffe, who turned away
to eat some leaves from
a tree.

"I'm going to be stuck with
dry grass forever," he grumbled.

And that is why giraffes are tall
and rhinos are so grumpy today.

The Goose that laid the Golden Eggs

Long ago, in a distant land, there
lived a poor man and his wife.

The man's
name was Tom...

...and his wife was called Elena.
They were very poor, but they had
everything they needed.

They had a goat
to give them milk.

And a
tabby cat to
keep them
company.

They had a garden to grow vegetables...

...and they had hens and geese
to lay fresh eggs for breakfast and
supper. So Tom and Elena were content.

Every morning, Tom got up
early and filled a basket with
just-laid eggs.

Then he set out
from their cottage to sell the
eggs at the local village market.

One morning, as Tom was collecting the eggs, he found something strange.

What's this?

One of the eggs was dark yellow and very, very heavy.

Tom was annoyed. He thought it had to be a trick. He raced outside, shouting for Elena.

"Look at this! Someone stole one of our eggs and left a stone in its place."

But Elena looked closer...

That's not a stone, Tom.

To her astonishment, Tom was holding a solid gold egg!

That day, Tom took all the
eggs to the market as usual.

Then he headed for the goldsmith to
show him the golden egg.

The goldsmith couldn't believe his eyes when Tom held up the egg.

"That's remarkable," he cried. "I'll buy it."

And he gave Tom a bag bulging with shiny gold coins.

Tom gasped. He had never seen so much money in his life.

Tom went straight back to the market and bought a beautiful silk dress for Elena.

Then he went home, thinking about how happy she would be when he gave her the dress.

As soon as he got home, he held out the dress proudly. But, to his disappointment, Elena wasn't happy at all. In fact, she looked annoyed.

"Oh Tom, it's far too good for me to wear," she snapped. "And we need to fix the roof."

Tom felt dreadful. Elena was right. He should have saved the money, instead of rushing out to spend it.

It was too late now – he had spent
every last coin on the dress. He sighed.

Then, the next morning, when Tom went to collect the eggs...

Look, another one!

...he found another golden egg, exactly like the first one.

And the morning after that, he found yet another. "It's the little white goose!" he said happily.

She must be a magic goose.

Every day, Tom sold a golden egg to the goldsmith.

He used the money to buy splendid new clothes for himself and Elena.

He built a bigger, grander house, with a bigger and better garden. Then he hired servants to look after the animals and tend the fruit and vegetables for him.

Tom and Elena were rich!

275

But, as they became richer, they also became greedier.

I want a HUGE house.

Very soon, one golden egg a day wasn't enough for them.

"There must be a way of getting more golden eggs," said Tom, one afternoon.

"If only that little white goose would lay faster," Elena murmured.

"I know!" she cried out. "Let's kill the goose. Then we can cut her open and get all the eggs at once."

We'll be the richest people in the world!

So Elena grabbed the goose,
and Tom killed it.

But when they opened up the goose...

...they found that there was no gold inside at all.

"What have we done?"
wailed Elena.

No more gold!

We'll be poor again!

They had been too greedy and now
they had lost everything.

Tom kept on collecting eggs every
morning. But he never found another
golden egg, as long as he lived.

The Fox and the Stork

Fox and Stork were the best of friends.
Or at least, they were most of the time...

There was just one problem.
Fox loved playing tricks.

Even when it seemed as if Fox was being friendly...

...he usually had a trick up his sleeve.

Fox was always trying to think up new tricks to play on his friend.

One day he had a brilliant idea. "This will be my best trick yet!" he smiled to himself.

The next morning, Fox met
Stork in the woods. "Are you free for supper
tonight?" he asked. "Come at eight."

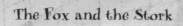

When Stork arrived,
Fox was cooking soup.

He poured it into
two flat bowls, and
a delicious smell
filled the room.

Stork was very
hungry. "Is it ready?"
she said. "Oh good!"

But, when she tried to
start, she was stuck. Her
long beak couldn't eat
from the wide, flat bowl.

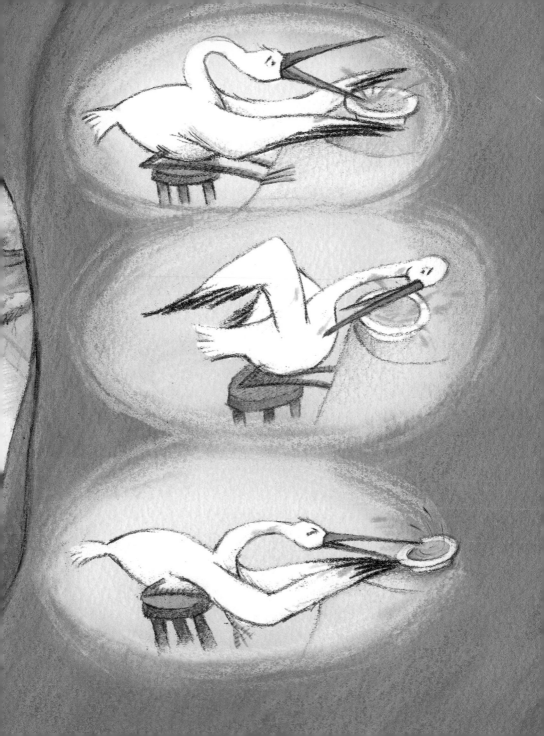

"Oh dear!" said Fox, laughing.
"Don't you like it?" And he poured
Stork's soup into his own bowl,
grinning at his cleverness.

I tricked
you!

Stork
didn't think
the trick
was very
funny.

The very next day,
she asked Fox to supper.

This time, Stork had planned
a trick of her own...

She made a delicious creamy soup, just like Fox. He smiled as he saw it, simmering on the stove. When it was ready, Stork poured it into tall, thin jars.

Fox pushed his short snout as far as he could into the jar. But he couldn't reach the soup.

"What's the matter?" asked Stork,
innocently. "Don't you like it?"

Fox sulked. "That was a rotten trick to play," he grumbled.

"I don't know why you're so cross. It's exactly the same trick you played on me," Stork pointed out.

"You have to be kind to your friends, if you want them to be kind to you," she added, as she cleared away the dishes.

"Maybe you'll think
twice before playing
another of your tricks."
    "Hmph," said Fox
and he headed –
hungrily – for home.

The Hare and the Tortoise

Harry Hare loved running
more than anything in the world.

Everyone said he was the fastest
hare around – maybe even the fastest
hare in history.

309

Every morning, he woke up
early and went for a long run.

Then he ran to work.

He ran all day,

and then he ran home.

Whenever he got a chance, Harry loved to show everyone just how fast he was.

In fact, running and speed
were all he ever talked about...

Well, of
course, I do a lot
of training.

Tom Tortoise worked with Harry. All day long, he heard Harry boasting. Tom didn't think Harry was so special.

I beat my own record – again!

Harry was always laughing at how slow Tom was. "Take your time, Tommy!" he joked.

I'll just jog here until you're ready!

One morning, Harry ran to work in record time. He was feeling especially pleased with himself.

I really need some extra heavy shoes to slow me down!

"I must be the fastest creature in the world," he boasted. "I know – let's have a race to prove it."

Come on, who wants to race me?

To everyone's surprise, Tom Tortoise plodded over. "I'll race you, Harry," he said.

"Tommy Slowcoach?
Are you serious?" laughed Harry.
"You wouldn't even get started!"

Ho ho, that's
a good one!

"I mean it," said Tom. "Let's have the race next Saturday at ten o'clock. You can choose where."

Well, we'll all have a good laugh anyway.

321

For the next few days, the animals talked about nothing else.

Have you heard about the race?

Has Tommy gone crazy?

The story was in all the newspapers.

It was even on television.

Harry began to train harder than ever.
He woke up extra early in the mornings,
and went running in the evenings too.

He was sure he would win, but he wanted to win by miles. He chose a good long course for the race.

Tom Tortoise didn't seem to be training at all. Perhaps he thought there was no point.

"Don't you think you should exercise a little?" asked Bob Badger. Tom simply smiled and had another cupcake.

The Hare and the Tortoise

At last, Saturday arrived. All Harry's friends came to watch him race.

Tom's friends were there too, but
they didn't look quite as happy.

It was a beautiful day. Harry saw some television cameras and did a little running especially for them.

"Hello everyone!" he called, and waved.

Tom just kept on talking
to his friends.

Soon it was time for the race to begin. Harry was already at the starting line, as Tom slowly ambled over.

Come on Tommy, let's not start late.

"On your marks, get set, GO!"
shouted the umpire.

Harry raced off and disappeared
at once. Everyone laughed as poor
Tom plodded slowly over the line.

As soon as he was out
of sight, Harry stopped beside
a tree to rest.

Just...
need to... catch...
my breath...

After all his early morning training, not to mention his late night runs, Harry was exhausted.

Besides, nobody
was looking. He had
plenty of time to sit
down for a while. He
would still win the
race easily.

His eyes started closing. "Perhaps I'll have a quick nap," he thought. "That will make it even funnier when I win the race."

Harry settled down in the shade.
Soon, he was fast asleep.

Meanwhile, Tom Tortoise was slowly but steadily making his way along the course.

Most of the animals had gone straight to the finish line. Tom's friends stayed with him, to cheer him on.

Nobody saw Harry sleeping under his tree.

341

Hours passed. The sun slipped down in the sky and the air grew cool.

Harry woke with a shiver.

He blinked his eyes sleepily...
and remembered the race! He
hadn't meant to sleep for so long.
Never mind, he was sure he
would still beat Tom.

And he felt much better
after his nap. He did a few
stretches, then raced off.

Soon he could see the finish line.
There was a huge crowd...

...and they were
already cheering.

At that moment he saw a small,
brown shell shape coming up to the line.

Harry felt cold all over.
Surely that couldn't be Tom?

347

He ran faster than ever before.
He was losing! The cheering grew
louder and louder.

Look,
it's Harry!

Whatever
happened to
him?

Harry dived over the line, but he was too late.

Well done Tommy!

Tom Tortoise had won the race – and he didn't even look out of breath.

Aesop

Four of the stories in this book
were taken from Aesop's* Fables. These
fables are a collection of short stories,
first told in ancient Greece around
4,000 years ago.

Nobody knows exactly who Aesop
was, but the stories are still popular
today, and they are known all
around the world.

The stories are often about animals
and they always have a "moral"
(a message or lesson) at the end.

* say Ee-sop's

The Brothers Grimm

"The Musicians of Bremen", also known as "The Town Musicians of Bremen", was first written down by two brothers, Jacob and Wilhelm Grimm.

The brothers lived in Germany over two hundred years ago. They collected old folk and fairy tales from all over Europe.

"The Town Musicians of Bremen" was first published in their book, "Children's and Household Tales".

Digital manipulation by John Russell

First published in 2008 by Usborne Publishing Ltd, 83-85 Saffron Hill,
London EC1N 8RT, England.
www.usborne.com Copyright © 2008 Usborne Publishing Ltd.
The name Usborne and the devices 🎈 🎈 are Trade Marks of Usborne Publishing Ltd.
First published in America in 2009. UE. Printed in China.